Snarlyhissopus

To the Burnsides, big and small – with love
A.M.

For Francesca Zannoni and Nik,
with love and thanks
L.V.

Scholastic Children's Books,
Commonwealth House, 1-19 New Oxford Street,
London WC1A 1NU, UK
a division of Scholastic Ltd
London ~ New York ~ Toronto ~ Sydney ~ Auckland
Mexico City ~ New Delhi ~ Hong Kong

First published in the UK in hardback by Scholastic Ltd, 2002
This paperback edition published by Scholastic Ltd, 2003

ISBN 0 439 98211 1

Printed by Oriental Press, Dubai, UAE

2 4 6 8 10 9 7 5 3 1

Snarlyhissopus

by
Alan MacDonald

illustrated by
Louise Voce

Hippo

One morning, Pelican met
a new animal in the jungle.
She had never seen
anything like it before.

"Hello," said Pelican.
"What sort of a thing are you?"

"I'm a hippopotamus,"
replied the hippopotamus.

Pelican flew off to tell Monkey.

"Guess what?
I've seen a strange new
animal," said Pelican.

"What is it?" asked Monkey.

Pelican tried to remember.
"It's a SPOTTYHIPPOMUS," she said.

Monkey
swung off
through
the trees and
found Zebra.

"Watch out,"
said Monkey.
"There's a
huge, ugly
creature heading
this way."

Zebra passed Leopard
sleeping in the shade.
"Run!" said Zebra,
"there's an enormous,
slimy beast and
it's chasing me."

"What is it?" asked Leopard.

"It's a DRIPASLOBBERMOUTH!"
said Zebra.

Leopard ran ahead
and told Ant-eater.

"What is it?" asked
Ant-eater fearfully.

"It's not safe, there's a hairy, hungry, snarling brute and I can hear it coming!"

"It's a
GRIPPERSNAPPERTOOTH!"

Ant-eater told the alarming news to Giraffe.

"Look out, there's a gigantic, pink jelly thing coming, and it will swallow you whole!"

"What is it?" asked Giraffe, trembling at the knees.

"It's a GULPAWOBBLETUSK!"

Giraffe found
Elephant taking
his nap.

"Wake up!
Wake up!"
panted Giraffe.
"A terrible,
roaring,
clawing,
wild-eyed
monster
is going to
gobble us
all up!"
Elephant
opened
one eye.
"What kind
of monster?"
he yawned.

"A SNARLYHISSOPUS!"

But Elephant waggled his great ears and said *he* wasn't scared of monsters.

He sent Giraffe to bring all the animals to the high hill. "Now listen, this is my clever plan," said Elephant. "We shall all hide, and when the monster comes we will . . .

. . . jump on it,

push it,

bump it

and shove it
downhill into
the muddy
brown creek.
That will teach
it a lesson."

All the animals agreed
this was a clever plan
and went to find a
hiding place.

After a little while,
they heard something
moving in the bushes.
The monster was coming!

On a signal from Elephant,
they all jumped on it. Pushing,
bumping and shoving with all their
might, they rolled the monster downhill
into the muddy brown creek.

splat!

Hippopotamus rolled over in the warm squelchy mud. "Mmmm, loverly!" she said. Elephant stared. "But *you're* not a monster! Where is the SNARLYHISSOPUS?"

"I think you're a bit muddled,"
Hippopotamus giggled.
"I'm a hippopotamus,
and hippopotamuses
simply love mud baths.
Have you ever tried one yourself?"

None of
them had.
So they all
jumped into
the muddy
brown creek.

And before
long, it was
hard to tell
which of
them was a
hippopotamus
and which
was a . . .

. . . WHAT-ON-EARTHAMUS!